MY MOUNTAIN MAN RESCUER

WILD HEART MOUNTAIN: MOUNTAIN HEROES

SADIE KING

MY MOUNTAIN MAN RESCUER

WILD HEART MOUNTAIN: MOUNTAIN HEROES

A secret billionaire mountain man and a curvy girl with a secret, stuck together on the side of a mountain...

I'm a volunteer for Wild Heart Mountain Search and Rescue, and when I find Chantelle injured on the side of the mountain, my world shifts.

I should take her to the medical center, but instead I take her to my cabin.

She's mine, and I won't give her up.

But Chantelle's hiding something, and I won't let her leave until I know all her secrets...

even if I won't tell her mine.

My Mountain Man Rescuer is a forced proximity, age gap, instalove romance featuring a secret billionaire hero and the curvy innocent woman who rescues his heart.

ALEX

The radio crackles to life just as I hang up my backpack. It's been a long few hours and my body is weary, but I'm the responder on call, so I pick up the radio and wait for it to crackle again.

I was called out this afternoon to look for a missing kid. Turns out he was waiting in the car for his parents all along wondering what all the flashing lights were for.

A missing kid gets every volunteer on both sides of the mountain out, and the Wild Heart Mountain Rescue hut is full of weary men and women in their high vis jackets.

Half of Fire and Rescue came to help the Mountain Rescue team, and I watch through the window as one of their fire wardens, Erika, speaks to the sheepish-looking parents.

The kid is in his mom's arms, clinging around her neck with his head resting on her chest. He looks peaceful and safe, and I smile at the touching scene of mother and child.

They move away, and Erika comes into the hut shaking her head.

"Stupid kids," she mumbles as she stomps over to the Fire and Rescue team.

"You coming for a drink or you heading to the gym?" one of the other fire volunteers asks.

Erika's known for the hours she puts in lifting at the gym. She's a big girl and strong, could lift more than half the guys here.

"I need a drink after that."

When we're all out, we work together, but the friendly rivalry between the two mountain EMS teams is obvious as soon as the job's done.

The Fire and Rescue team stands on one side of the hut and the Search and Rescue team on the other. Then there's me, in the dark corner on my own, where I prefer to be.

"Base to Responder One, are you receiving?"

Suzie's voice crackles through the radio, and I push the speaker button.

"Responder One, here."

"We might have another call out."

I glance around the hut. The other volunteers look

weary. It's almost dark out and they're chatting amiably, no doubt looking forward to a beer.

All I'm looking forward to is a warm fire and the solitude of my cabin.

"I'll take it. Coming through."

I stride across the hut to the door that leads to the comms room. Symon follows me. As a park ranger, he likes to know everything that happens on Wild Heart Mountain. A few of the other guys break away from the group, and we all head to the comms room.

Suzie swivels in her office chair as we walk in. Behind her is a bank of computers and one other volunteer manning the phones, his headset pressed to his head.

In the corner, a playpen houses her toddler. The little guy sits among a pile of soft toys stacking colorful blocks. Suzie can't always find a sitter while she's working, and he's become a feature of the place. No one's going to tell a single mom she can't bring her kid to work occasionally and especially not Suzie.

"This might be a hoax, or we've got a missing hiker. A girl hasn't come back."

I glance out the window at the fading light. At this time of year, the temperature drops as soon as the sun sets. Anyone still on the trails is going to feel that chill.

"Another kid?" Symon asks.

There's a sharp edge of concern in his voice. The

man's got a young family, and any time a kid goes missing it gets him in a way I don't yet understand.

Suzie shakes her head. "I say girl. She's a woman, a young woman who set out from town to walk the Mid Peak trail."

"Was she on her own?" I ask.

It's supposed to be empowering, but I hate the thought of young women hiking these trails on their own. There're more than bears out there that can hurt you.

Suzie frowns. "That's the odd thing. The caller was evasive. It was kind of weird."

"Weird how?"

The back of my neck prickles uneasily. We're trained for all scenarios. Half the team are ex-military, and you never know who might be on the mountain and what their agenda is.

Suzie bites her lower lip, thinking. "It's probably better if I play it to you."

She swivels back to her computer and a few moments later has the call on speaker.

A man's voice croaks through the speakers.

"There's a girl on the…um…Mid Peak trail. She… um…she hasn't come back."

The voice trails off, and Suzie speaks. "What's her name, sir?"

"Chantelle. She didn't come back."

"So Chantelle is the girl's name. When you say girl, how old is she?"

"Umm, twenty-one, maybe twenty-two…"

I catch Symon's eye, and he looks as skeptical as I feel. It sounds like a hoax. The guy's uncertain, and he's not giving any information about himself.

The call goes on for another twenty seconds or so as Suzie tries to get more details. But all we get is that a woman is still on the Mid Peak trail and she may be hurt.

The recording finishes, and Suzie swivels around again to face us.

"It could be a hoax…" She shrugs her shoulders.

"Or there could be an injured woman on the Mid Peak trail," I finish.

Dusk is closing in fast. If this woman, Chantelle, is up there, then we need to find her before dark or our job gets a lot harder.

The Mid Peak trail starts in town, which makes it popular with day hikers. It heads almost straight up the mountain to a lookout point over the valley before looping back.

"I'll take the Jeep up to the ridge and cut into the trail from there."

It's already been a long afternoon, but if there's a chance someone's out there who needs help, then there's only one thing to do.

"I'll start at the base of the trail," says Zach, one of the other volunteers.

Symon barks orders to a few of the other guys, but I'm already slipping my backpack back on.

If there's a woman hurt out there, I need to move fast. I hate the thought of anyone being out on the mountain injured and especially a young woman in the dark.

I hear Symon calling the Sheriff as I leave. The call in sounded dodgy as fuck, and if it's a hoax and wasting all our time, then the little shit who called it in should get dealt with by the law.

2

ALEX

"Chantelle!" I call into the darkness.

Shadows loom across the trail and skitter away when my flashlight beam glides over them.

I stop to listen in case anyone calls out for help. But the only sounds are insects chirping and small animals scurrying into the undergrowth.

The noise I'm making should be enough to scare off any bears or wild cats, but I keep my hunting rifle slung over my shoulder just in case.

"Chantelle!"

I get moving again, spurred on by the thought of some lost soul on the side of the mountain.

"It's Search and Rescue. If you can hear me, call out!"

There's no response and I keep going, moving my flashlight methodically from side to side as I go.

I come to a rocky outcrop where boulders stack up on either side of the trail. It's a beautiful spot in the daylight with a view over the valley, a popular photo stop. Tourists used to be content with taking a photo of just the vista, but these days, they want to be in it too, a selfie with the view. They'll climb further and further onto the boulders trying to get the perfect shot for social media.

Last year, a woman fell to her death trying to capture the perfect video.

I shuffle to the edge of the boulder and shine the flashlight into the valley. A small animal darts out of the way of the flashlight as my beam sweeps over foliage and large boulders. No bodies. But that doesn't mean she's not down there.

If we don't find the girl by the morning and Symon thinks the call wasn't a hoax, we'll come back and search the valley.

It's as I step back from the boulder that my flashlight picks up a streak of red. Blood on the side of a small boulder.

"Chantelle!"

It could be animal blood or it could be from a missing woman.

"This is Search and Rescue, can you hear me?"

The moan is so soft I almost miss it. A feminine moan that under other circumstances might make a man's blood run hot.

I pivot quickly and retrace my steps off the boulder and to the other side of the trail. There's an arrangement of boulders here and one of them juts out, balanced above the others.

My flashlight sweeps the area, and that's when I see her.

A woman, huddled in the crevice of where two boulders meet. Her knees are scraped with blood and dirt. She's wearing cut off jean shorts, and so help me God, but I can't help noticing her thick, creamy thighs that she's hugging to her chest.

In one hand she's clasping bear spray, and when her eyes meet mine, they're frightened. Two wide blue discs full of pain and terror.

"Chantelle?"

I crouch down in front of her, and she looks at me warily. Her mouth opens and closes a few times like she's trying to make it work. Her lips are chapped and dusted with dirt, but I can tell they're usually full and plump. Dark hair frames her face and falls in waves down her shoulders.

She's beautiful. Even dehydrated, scraped, and dirty, one look at her stirs my soul.

"Yes," she whispers.

I grab the water bottle from the side of my backpack.

"I'm Alex from Wild Heart Mountain Search and Rescue."

I keep my tone reassuring, like I've been trained, as I press the water bottle to her lips. She parts her lips like a kitten trying to feed and her head tilts back, showing the curve of her neck as her hair cascades over her shoulders.

God help me. She's dehydrated and injured, and all I can think about is grabbing her hair in my fist and kissing her dirt-stained lips.

I'm a bad man, and I need to focus.

"Are you injured?"

She nods slowly, and I'm reminded again of a kitten, wide eyed and uncertain.

"Where abouts?"

She shows me her arm where there's a few scrapes and her knees. It doesn't look too bad. Only one scrape is deep with a trickle of blood and is probably where the blood on the boulder came from. They'll need cleaning out and dressing.

"Anything else?"

"My ankle." She unhooks her legs and stretches them out in front of her. Long thick legs that I'd love to run my hands up. "I think it's sprained."

She's got a pair of sneakers on her feet. Urban

sneakers not even the type you do sports in. The laces are frayed, and the left one has a hole in the place where the edging meets the fabric. They're totally unsuitable for the mountain.

But this isn't the time to lecture her about the appropriateness of her footwear. My job here is to find the missing woman and get her to safety. To take her to the medical center in Hope for a checkup.

But as I look at her kitten face, her luscious curves, and the way she's looking at me like I'm her savior, a fierce wave of protectiveness rushes over me.

There's no way I'm handing Chantelle over to the care of someone else.

This woman is mine. I found her; I'm keeping her.

I can't tell much about the ankle in the dark, but once I get her back to my place, I can get ice on it and check it out properly.

"Can you walk?"

She shakes her head. "I'm not sure."

"I'm going to help you to your feet."

My arm slides around her waist. She's a thick girl, and I like the feel of her as she leans her body against mine. If only she wasn't so damn cold. She's shivering against me.

A million questions run through my mind. What's she doing out on the trail in nothing but short shorts and flimsy sneakers? What happened to her, and who's the guy who called in because she was missing?

If that was her boyfriend, I'll personally hunt the fucker down myself. No one leaves a woman alone on the side of a mountain and especially an injured one.

But there will be time for questions later. My first concern is treating her wounds and getting her warm.

I help Chantelle to her feet, and as soon as she puts weight on her left foot, a grimace of pain crosses her face.

"Definitely sprained," she whispers, her voice still not working properly.

It'll make it difficult for her to walk back to my Jeep, but I've got a solution for that.

"Do you have a backpack?"

I sweep my flashlight around the area, but she shakes her head. Who comes out hiking with no backpack? At least she had bear spray. But why that and nothing else? I wonder when she last ate and how long she's been sitting in the cold.

Anger flares in me at whoever that asshole was who called this in.

Chantelle leans against me, unable to balance on her own, and as I breathe in her honey and lavender scent, my chest pinches and the protective feeling grows stronger.

This woman has been left all alone, but she's my

responsibility now. I'll look after her. I'll take care of her.

My radio crackles, and Symon's voice comes over the waves.

"Any luck, Responder One?"

I should have called in the moment I found her. I should have let the team know. But there's something about Chantelle that makes me want to keep her to myself.

"I've found her."

Symon gives a sigh of relief, and I explain her injuries and the state she's in.

"I'll call ahead to the medical center and let them know she's on her way."

"No."

The forcefulness of my voice makes my kitten look up at me with curiosity.

"She's potentially dehydrated. My place is close. I'll take her there and dress the injuries myself."

Symon is silent on the other end of the radio. It's an unusual course of action but not unreasonable. It could take another forty minutes to get to Hope from up here, but we'll be at my cabin in ten minutes.

"It's unusual, Alex."

"I'm taking her to my place." My voice is firm, and Symon must hear something in my tone because he doesn't argue. Maybe he knows exactly how I feel.

Rumor has it he practically kidnapped his wife the night they first met.

"I'll get Sheriff to drop by. He'll want to know what happened up there."

He leaves the rest unsaid, that it might be foul play, that they need to find out who the man is who called it in and see if we're dealing with an assault.

I end the radio call. Because I don't want to think of someone coming for my kitten. She's mine now. I know it in my bones, and I'll do anything to keep her with me.

Shouldering my backpack and gun, I slide one arm behind her thighs and lift her into my arms.

Chantelle lets out a little sigh and her head drops against my chest. A few moments later, she's fast asleep.

3

CHANTELLE

The man picks me up as if I'm not a chubby girl whose exhaustion is making her a dead weight. I try to keep my head up, but I'm so tired it droops against his chest.

He smells earthy, like pines and dirt. The beat of his heart is reassuring in its steady rhythm as he carries me down the winding trail. He's sturdy and warm and *safe,* and I sag into him.

My eyelids are heavy, and I'll just rest them for a moment...

When I wake up, I'm in a strange room. Soft pillows prop me up and I must be in a hospital, but the bed covers are navy and thick and there's no sterile smell.

In fact, it smells like wood smoke and pine, and the scent of the man still lingers in the air.

"You're awake."

I turn my head to the sound of the voice, and the man . . . what did he say his name was? Alfie or Alan is sitting in an armchair next to the bed watching me.

"Where am I?" Because it sure as hell isn't a hospital.

"You're in my cabin. It was closer to bring you here."

He's watching me closely, and I try to remember the last few hours. There's a bandage on my arm, but I have no recollection of it getting there.

"You passed out," he continues. "I brought you back here and dressed your arm. You didn't even wake up."

That explains it. But it's disconcerting, especially when I look down and I'm not in the t-shirt I was wearing this morning.

"Where are my clothes?"

I press the front of the t-shirt, and there's no bra underneath. I glance up at the man, and he's watching me with a blank expression.

"Your clothes were filthy, and there was blood on them."

Now that I really look at him, I notice the deep grey of his eyes and the small lines around the edges.

His dark hair is streaked with silver as is his shaggy beard. He's got to be at least a decade older than me, but he's hot. Like capital H. HOT.

The thought of him undressing me when I was unconscious causes a flicker of heat between my legs.

"Did you…" My cheeks heat at the thought of him seeing me naked.

The man chuckles, and the laugh makes his eyes twinkle in a way that animates his entire face.

"Relax, kitten. My housekeeper dressed you. Your virtue is intact."

I look away quickly so he doesn't see my disappointment. Which is crazy. Since when did I ever want a stranger to see me naked?

"I've got chicken soup. It should still be warm."

At the mention of food, my stomach lets out an unladylike growl. I haven't eaten since the picnic I packed for lunch. Which makes me think of how hopeful I was this morning as I spread butter on the last four slices of bread, starting to turn in the plastic packet. Humming to myself thinking about how the day would go.

Memory from the afternoon floods my mind, and I push it away. I'm not ready to think about it yet, to think about how stupid my scheme was. How I utterly failed, again.

I pull myself up in the bed and wince when pain shoots up my ankle.

"Don't try to move too much, kitten. Your ankle's sprained, and I haven't wrapped it yet."

There's a tray of food on the nightstand by the bed, and he hands me a glass of orange juice as he transfers himself from the chair to the side of the bed. I gulp if down until he takes the glass off me.

"Whoa. Go easy with that. We need to get your fluid intake up slowly, okay?"

I nod, because with the basic first aid I've done I know he's right.

"What's the time?" I'm disoriented and don't know how long I was out. My brain isn't ready to think about what happened. But I can try to make sense of the here and now.

"It's after 8 P.m. I found you about an hour ago.

He found me. Shame flares in my cheeks. It was stupid to venture into the mountain, to think that a walk in nature would change anything. The healing power of forest bathing and all that. Look where it got me.

The man brings a spoonful of soup to my lips, and there's no way to do this elegantly but to slurp. He doesn't seem to mind and carefully holds up another spoonful.

Chunks of chicken and carrot with a spicy kick to

it make my taste buds come to life. It's the best meal I've eaten in weeks. I can feel it warming me up and healing me already.

He feeds me a few more spoonfuls before he takes the bowl away.

"A little bit at a time, just to make sure your stomach can handle it."

I don't know why he's looking after me the way he is, but it feels good to have someone take care of my basic needs.

"Are you a doctor?"

He shakes his head. "No. I'm Alex, from Search and Rescue."

Alex. I commit the name to memory while Alex feeds me a few more mouthfuls of soup.

"In a few minutes the Park Ranger and the Sheriff will be here, and they're going to want to ask you some questions."

Panic rises in my chest. I'm not ready to answer questions and least of all to the authorities. The man's watching me closely, and I'm too late to hide my worried expression.

He puts a hand on mine. It's supposed to be reassuring, but the heat coming from him causes a delicious skitter across my skin, a spark where he's touching me.

"You're not in any trouble, Chantelle."

It's not me that I'm worried about, but I don't tell the kind stranger that.

"They're good guys. They're just trying to get a picture of what happened on the mountain and to get you any more help if you need it."

A picture of what happened on the mountain. I was a trusting dumbass, again, and got myself in trouble, again. There's no way I can tell the authorities the truth or this kind stranger. I wonder if he'd still let me between his clean Egyptian cotton sheets if he knew the truth about me.

He holds up the bowl of soup and spoons a bit more into my mouth while I try to think about what I can tell the Sheriff.

I'm angry at myself for getting sucked in again. I should go after Chris; I should stop him from doing what he's so desperate to do. But it's dark outside, and I'm on the side of a mountain with a sprained ankle.

There's nothing I'll be able to do tonight anyway. It's best if I stay here if I can and find a way to make this right tomorrow. I've got a bed for the night and a hot meal. I can slip out early tomorrow and find Chris. At least I'm not in a hospital where I would have to wait to be discharged. It should be easy to leave this cabin when I need to.

There's the sound of voices from outside the door, and the man gets up from the bed.

"Are you ready to see them?"

I take in a deep breath and force a smile.

"Yes." My voice is raspy, a pitiful croak that I hate the sound of, but it might just serve me well for the lie I'm about to tell.

"Bring them in."

4
ALEX

Chantelle looks tiny sitting up in the double king size bed, the covers smoothed out around her like a calm sea. My kitten is tired but wary as she steels herself for the questions that need to be asked.

I'm dying of curiosity as to what her story is but have kept my mouth shut until now. She needed medical attention first and a good meal second.

I would have liked to question her on my own, but the boys are here now and there's no reason not to let them in.

There's every chance they'll insist she goes to the medical center in Hope, but I won't let that happen. I've already got a doctor on the way. I paid her an exorbitant amount to make this house call in a remote part of the mountain at this time of night, but it will be worth it if means keeping Chantelle under my roof.

Symon and Calvin stride into the room, each man is as broad and imposing as I am. My kitten practically shrinks before them.

I drag an extra chair to the side of the bed and indicate for the men to sit down. I stay at the head of the bed, pacing. Ready to stop the questions if they get to be too much for Chantelle.

"I'm Sheriff Reid," says Calvin. "And this is Symon, the Head Ranger."

Her gaze darts between them, and she licks her lips nervously.

"How are you feeling?" asks Calvin.

She seems to relax at the gentle tone, hopefully realizing these guys are on her side. I've worked with Calvin and Symon long enough to understand the responsibility they both feel for the people on the mountain.

"Okay." She nods her head. "My ankle's sprained, but I'm feeling okay."

Symon looks concerned. "Do you know how long you were out there? I'm trying to get a picture of if you might be dehydrated."

She bites her lower lip. "I had a water bottle in my backpack…"

There was no backpack when I found her, and she

hasn't mentioned one before. Unless it went off the side of the rocks.

"She's had juice and soup since she woke up," I interject. If I thought Chantelle was in any real medical danger, I'd take her to the medical center, but I'm pretty sure she's fine. Shaken, but fine.

"Can you tell us what happened out there?" Calvin asks.

She swallows hard, and her eyes dart to mine before she looks down. When she speaks, it's so quiet I move to the end of the bed to hear better.

"I tripped and fell."

Calvin leans forward, trying to hear her better too.

"You tripped?"

She nods. "I wasn't paying attention on the boulders."

She lifts her wide eyes to him, but the look is a little too intense.

She's lying.

"Were you on your own?"

"Yeah." Chantelle nods and looks away.

Calvin frowns, and we share a look. Someone radioed her in. Someone else was there.

"What happened to the guy you were with?"

She looks up quickly, a startled look in her eyes. "I was on my own."

Calvin takes a notebook out of his pocket and

checks his notes. Chantelle's gaze follows the notepad, and she swallows nervously.

"We had a call in from a man at about 6:15 p.m. saying there was an injured woman on the Mid Peak trail. That's how we knew where to find you."

Her gaze meets mine, and it's clear she doesn't want to answer the question. I'm not sure what she's hiding or who she's protecting, but I won't have her stressed out anymore.

"That's enough for tonight."

My voice is firm, and Calvin gives me a raised eyebrow look. I meet his gaze, not backing down. He's a friend, and I get that he has a job to do, but I won't have anyone stressing out my kitten.

He sighs and puts his notebook away.

"We need to get you to the Hope Medical center. I'd like you to get looked over properly to check for signs of dehydration or exposure."

"Dr. Ryder is on her way." Both Symon and Calvin stare at me. "Chantelle stays here."

Symon has a knowing look, but Calvin's frowning. It's his job to be suspicious, so I don't blame him. He hasn't worked it out yet. Chantelle's mine.

He turns back to Chantelle.

"Have you called your people to let them know you're safe? Is someone coming to get you?"

Calvin asks the questions I've been too afraid to ask.

I don't want to hear that Chantelle's burly boyfriend is coming to collect her, although if he does, I'll give him a dressing down for letting her hike on her own. But if he was the one who left her stranded, then I'll take him into the wilderness and make it look like a bear got him.

Chantelle shakes her head. "My phone…it was in the backpack."

"And you don't have the backpack anymore?" he asks gently.

"No."

Damn. I must have missed it on the trail. "I'll go out at first light and see if I can find it for you."

She shakes her head quickly. "It's not there."

We all look at her, and she bites her lower lip. It looks like she wants to take her words back.

"I…um…I think I was mugged."

Her eyes dart away as she says it. It's a lie, for sure. But Calvin sits back down and takes his notebook out again.

"You were mugged, huh?"

She nods. "Yeah. I guess that explains the guy calling it in." She shrugs her shoulders like that's one mystery all wrapped up.

Calvin asks a few more questions and takes some notes, but no one's buying it. No one gets mugged on the side of a mountain. She's protecting someone, and I'm determined to find out who.

"Do you want to use my phone to call someone?" Symon asks. "Is there someone who will come and get you?"

She shakes her head, and her eyes find mine. Her expression is worried, but there's hope in them when they land on me.

"Can I? Um…can I stay here tonight?"

Her cheeks flame at having to ask, and I sit on the bed next to her. "Kitten, you can stay here as long as you need."

Symon chortles behind me, but I don't care. I've found my woman, and once I find out what the fuck is going on with her, I'll make sure she's safe and I'll protect her for the rest of my days.

Calvin eyes me long and hard. "It's not orthodox to keep a rescue in your cabin, Alex."

She's not just a rescue, she's my future. I feel it in my bones.

"Is she under arrest?"

"No, but she needs to see a doctor."

"And I've got a doctor coming."

He clenches his jaw. "She should go home to her people and get looked after at home."

He's right. I'm being a selfish asshole insisting she stay. But when I glance at the woman in the bed, my heart clenches at her frailty. I am a selfish bastard.

"Can I speak to you outside?" His voice is tight and it makes me uneasy, but I guess he's just doing his job. I follow him into the hallway, along with Symon, and pull the door shut behind us.

"You heard her say she's got no people, Calvin. She wants to stay. It's not against the law to have a willing guest in my house."

He stares me down.

"It's not against the law, but if I find out you've taken advantage of a vulnerable woman on my mountain, I'll string you up myself."

And that's why I like Calvin. Because he cares. He feels his responsibility for every soul on this mountain and especially the vulnerable ones.

It's also shit that my reputation still lingers, even though it's been seven years since I left my old life and old reputation behind.

"I won't take advantage of her."

Not until she begs me to, I think silently. Because the Sheriff reads me right. It's for selfish reasons I want to keep Chantelle here. I want to do all the things to her he fears I'll do. But I'm a patient man. I'll wait until she's recovered, and she feels it too.

"I just want to look after her as much as you do.

Miriam, my housekeeper is here. She can play chaperone if it makes you feel any better. But I'm not sending her away until she's ready."

We're eyeing each other, Calvin no doubt weighing how much he thinks he knows me. What he knows of me from living on the mountain the last seven years versus what he read about me in the tabloids before that.

The last few years must mean something, because he gives me a grim nod.

"Fine." He lets out a long breath. "But watch your back until we find out who the fuck the mystery guy is, because I don't believe she was mugged."

"I want updates on anything you find about him."

He nods, and the tension goes out of the air, and we're just three guys again trying to keep people safe.

Only Chantelle isn't just anyone. She's mine, and I don't know how the fuck to explain that to anyone, least of all myself.

Symon slaps me on the shoulder.

"I'll book my tux for the wedding."

He smirks at me, the knowing smile of a man who's been there.

I shake my head. "Fuck off, the both of you."

They take their leave, Symon smiling like the fucking Cheshire Cat and Calvin scowling at me like a worried big brother.

Yeah, those boys know me too well.

Because they're both right. Chantelle is mine, and I want to do *all* the dirty things to her.

5

CHANTELLE

My ears strain in the silence, listening to the sounds of the cabin. The silence is unnerving. The only sounds come from outside, the wind rustling the trees and the occasional owl calling into the darkness.

When the doctor came earlier, she offered me painkillers to help me sleep. But I know better than that.

I need to stay alert and sharp. I took a couple of Advil for my ankle and slept anyway. The quiet of the cabin and the soft sheets pulling me under in a deep sleep like I haven't had in years.

The soft glow of the bedside clock tells me it's 5:15 a.m., just before dawn.

It's cozy in the bed, warm and safe. Alex has been kind to me and it would be easy to stay in bed, to be looked after for once in my life instead of being the one looking after somebody else. But that somebody else needs me.

I have to go now, before daybreak, before the household wakes up.

I sit up in bed and tear the blankets off me. The cold morning air makes my skin pimple. It's like a band aid ripping off, getting out of this soft warm bed, but it has to be done.

When my foot touches the floor, sharp pain shoots up my leg, and I clench my jaw to stop from calling out.

It hurts more than I realized, but I have to keep going. Putting my weight on the bedside table, I lift myself out of bed.

This time when I put my foot to the ground I test it first, finding where I need to put the weight to cause the least pain. If I put the weight on the ball of my foot with it tilted to the right, I can just about hobble.

The first place I go is to the window.

I pull back the thick curtain and gasp at the view. It's just before daylight, and the sky has a tinge of grey to it. Dark mountain peaks rise in the distance and below me dark shapes that can only be trees.

I really am in the middle of nowhere.

I tug at the latch and the window opens, letting in a blast of cool mountain air that make me shiver.

I don't have a sweater; I don't have anything but the oversized t-shirt Alex lent me.

My heart sinks. How am I going to get to the train station in nothing but a t-shirt and with a sprained ankle?

I didn't realize how remote this place is. Walking out of here might not be an option. But I have to try. If I stay any longer, Alex is going to ask me questions that I don't want to answer.

He's looked after me and he's being patient, but I'm on borrowed time. The Sheriff could be back today, and the last thing I need is getting noticed by the authorities.

I stick my head out the window and look down to a sheer drop. The cabin is right on the edge of a ravine with a stream running below.

To the left and right, the cabin extends on both sides. If you can even call this a cabin. Sure, it's made of wood, and it's in a forest and literally on the side of a mountain, but it's huge. Like, mansion size. Rooms extend on both sides with a balcony on the bottom floor that juts out over the ravine.

Maybe Alex brought me to a hotel. Surely a home this big can't be all for one person.

I close the window and hobble to the door.

It opens with a creak, and I peer out into a long

corridor with polished wooden floors and doors on either side.

I take a right, and leaning on the wall for support, drag my aching ankle down the hallway.

I pass several doorways adjacent to each other. If they're all bedrooms, then he must have a lot of guests or a big family.

I imagine Alex behind one of the doors, lying in a huge king-sized bed. And wonder if he sleeps naked.

The thought of the cool sheets plastered against his hard body has me heating up all over.

At the end of the hallway, there's a spiral staircase. Hanging on to the railing, I manage to get myself down it one painful step at a time.

On the bottom floor, the stairway opens up to a wide entryway. There's an open door to the left, and I peer in to find a massive brick fireplace at one end and a comfortable array of couches. It looks cozy in here. And I can imagine Alex sipping expensive whiskey with his rich friends in front of a roaring fire.

It's a different kind of life, one where I don't belong.

The opposite way leads to the kitchen, but it's bigger than any kitchen I've seen in my life.

A large granite counter takes up most of the space with stools placed around it.

There's a huge dining table and another set of

couches facing outwards. The predawn light tinges the sky grey, and I can make out the shape of the mountains. The view looks over the ravine, and it takes my breath away.

I stop for a minute, taking in my surroundings. Wondering who the hell Alex is and how much money does he have to be able to live like this.

The front door is probably alarmed, so I go through the scullery door of the kitchen to a walk-in pantry that's bigger than the last bedroom I had.

Beyond the pantry there's a corridor, and the doors here are open to a laundry that's, again, bigger than my last bedroom and a store cupboard.

There's a door at the back that leads down a couple of steps and to a garage.

A large four-wheel drive Jeep takes up a lot of space, as well as a little sports car. There's a huge Harley Roadster motorbike and a little 50cc scooter.

It's vintage and reminds me of the one that my mom used to own. I run my hand over the bright red vinyl seat, remembering the times when the three of us used to pile on. Me, Mom, and Chris. There were no helmets and Chris would go in the middle, being the youngest, sandwiched between me and Mom.

We'd go to the convenience store and pile the basket in front with groceries.

Once Mom got sick, I'd go myself and fill the

basket with a sixteen-year-old's version of groceries. A loaf of bread, a jar of peanut butter, apples if we could afford them, instant noodles when they were on sale.

What would Mom think now if she saw me in a place like this? Sleeping on Egyptian cotton sheets and being hand fed homemade soup.

She'd tell me to get my ass back up to bed and enjoy it for a few days. But that's because she doesn't know where my brother is.

Thinking about Chris gives me renewed energy. I've got to get out of this place. I've got to find him.

There's a door at the side of the garage that looks like it leads outside. I'm about to hobble over when a firm arm grips me around the wrist.

I scream as I spin around with my fist lashing out. It connects to something solid, and a man grunts. A light switch is flicked, and the place is flooded with light. I blink in the brightness and find myself face to face with Alex.

He's rubbing his jaw with one hand, and the other is still gripping my wrist.

"What the fuck? You scared me."

My heart's racing, and I don't know if it's because I've missed my chance to escape or I've been caught snooping, or if it's because of the hot man who's holding me who I just punched in the face.

"You've got a strong right hook."

I've had to learn to defend myself, but I don't tell Alex that. The realization of what I've done makes my heart sink. He'll throw me out for sure, but isn't that what I want?

"Sorry," I mumble.

He looks amused rather than angry, and I guess I need to practice my punches more.

"You should be resting."

His voice is firm, commanding, and I feel the pull of the soft bed and good food. But I'm not his prisoner here.

"I need to go."

He shakes his head. "You're not going anywhere on that ankle, kitten. I thought I told you to stay in bed."

His eyes flash dangerously. He's a man who's used to getting what he wants.

"Can't I leave?"

His left eye twitches in an expression I can't read. For a moment he seems hurt, but that doesn't make sense.

"If there's somewhere you need to be, tell me where and who will look after you, and I'll drop you off."

I stay silent.

There's nowhere he can drop me off that I want him to see. This guy lives in a mansion. He calls it a cabin, but just because it's made out of wood doesn't make it any less than a mansion.

Besides, who else is there to look after me?

"I can look after myself."

He smiles. "I don't doubt that for a second. But you're not going anywhere unless you can walk on that ankle, kitten."

I stare at him. Who the heck does he think he is telling me what to do? But at the same time, I'm also thinking about how nice it is to be looked after.

Now that the adrenaline has worn off, the throbbing of my ankle is intense. I didn't realize the pressure I've been putting on it sneaking around the house. Now that I've stopped, it feels like my whole leg's on fire. The pain creeps up my body, and I feel woozy.

I take a step backwards and accidentally put pressure on my foot.

A gasp slips out, and I wince in pain.

But Alex is there, anticipating my every move. Once more, he scoops me into his arms.

"Oh, kitten. When are you going to learn to stay put?"

His voice is gentle, and I put my arms around his neck. I barely know this man but he feels safe, reassuring.

Our faces are inches apart. He looks at me with intensity, and his lips brush mine. It's soft, but the heat from him travels all down my body.

"Let me take care of you, Chantelle."

My mouth searches for his, wanting to feel his lips on me. They're there, warm and reassuring, a sturdy life raft in the chaos of my life. I cling to him for one long, slow, lingering kiss before he pulls back.

He's kind and gentle, and he wants to take care of me. It's everything I've been missing in my life.

I want to help Chris, but Alex's right. I'm useless until I can walk, and that won't happen unless I rest.

I make a silent vow to help Chris when I can. But to help him, I need to heal myself.

Alex is offering to take care of me, and in that moment I surrender. I lean my head against his solid chest and let him carry me to my room.

6

CHANTELLE

*A*lex carries me back to bed, and I take another couple of Advil for the pain. Dawn light is turning the day grey, but I fall back asleep as soon as I'm tucked between the sheets.

He didn't kiss me again, even though I was longing for him to. I can't explain what I'm feeling towards him. After so long of taking care of other people, it feels so good to be taken care of.

My thoughts go to Chris, to what he might be doing without me to keep an eye on him. After what he did to me, I shouldn't care. But he's my brother. I'll always care. Besides, I made a promise to Mom before she passed that I would look after my little brother. I've failed her. For the last two years, I've failed her big time.

Maybe Alex is right. I need to rest and heal, and

what better place to do it than in an oversized cabin on the side of a mountain.

There's a knock at the bedroom door, and my heart skips a beat. I can still feel his lips on mine from the soft kiss last night. It was just a brush of the lips, barely a kiss, but it's left me wanting more.

I run a hand through my hair and sit up in bed, smoothing down my t-shirt.

"Come in."

A wide smile plasters my face, but it freezes when a middle-aged woman comes into the room. She's short and stout, wearing a plain grey tunic and a cheerful smile.

"I'm Miriam, the housekeeper."

The smell of bacon emanates from the tray she's carrying, and I try not to show disappointment as she brings it over.

"Alex asked me to make sure you're comfortable today."

I sit up in bed as she sets the tray down, wincing as my ankles catches on the bedsheets.

"Is he not home today?"

I try to keep my voice steady to hide my disappointment. Miriam shakes her head. "He had to pop out this morning. He'll be back later."

She bustles about the room, pulling back the curtains, and I blink in the bright light.

The bedside clock says almost ten. I never sleep this late, but a check in with Miriam lets me know it's accurate.

"I'll leave you alone to eat your breakfast, and I'll be back in half an hour to help you dress."

I'm about to tell her I have nothing to change into when she comes back into the room with a garment rack full of clothing.

"Alex asked me to pick some clothes up on the way in. I hope these are all right."

My mouth drops open. There are dresses on the rack and leggings and t-shirts all with tags hanging off them.

"Whose are these?" I whisper.

She gives me a smile like I'm a slow child. "They're yours now, love. I picked them up from the boutique in town. I hope that's all right. They're a bit bohemian, but it was the only thing that was open on my way through this morning."

She eyes me up and down with an assessing gaze. "Alex guessed at your size, so we'll see what fits."

My mouth drops open, speechless. "I can't afford these. You have to take them back."

Miriam chuckles. "It's no good telling Alex that. He's bought them now, love."

"But…" Panic rises in me. This is too much, too

generous. There must be a catch. "I can't pay him back."

She shakes her head. "I'm guessing he doesn't want you to, love. He's generous, and lord knows he can afford it. My advice? Enjoy the clothes while you can."

Miriam closes the door quietly behind her, and I'm left wondering, not for the first time, who the hell Alex is.

True to her word, Miriam reappears half an hour later to collect my breakfast tray and help me into the shower.

Any modesty I had disappears with her efficiency. She has me undressed and sitting on a stool in the shower before I can raise any complaints about her seeing me naked.

After the shower, she dresses my ankle, and I select a plain t-shirt and long skirt from the clothing. The fabric is soft, organic cotton, much nicer than the cheap clothing I'm used to.

I choose a grey waterfall cardigan that swishes around my hips. It is all a bit bohemian like Miriam warned, making me feel even more like a different person. But I like it, the way the fabric falls and the soft noises it makes as it brushes against my skin.

Miriam chats away as she dresses me. She lives in

Hope and has two almost grown up sons. Her oldest boy has just left for college, and the youngest one is going into the military. She speaks with pride about her sons, and I warm to her.

She brushes my hair and ties it back in a complicated plait. Her fingers are quick and strong, and my chest squeezes remembering how Mom used to plait my hair when I was a girl.

It makes me ache for my mother, the times with her and all the moments she's missed.

Once I'm dressed, Miriam brings in a pair of crutches for me.

"I've been instructed not to let you go too far; you have to rest. So I'll show you the library and the games room, and you should find something to entertain yourself."

I hobble after her, the crutches squeaking on the wooden floor.

We go left down the corridor, and she stops opposite a large double door.

"Do you like to read, Chantelle?"

Reading is a luxury I haven't had time for since Mom passed.

"I used to," I say, remembering more innocent days when I'd sprawl out in the spot where the sun came through the window on the faded carpet with a book from the library, the pages yellow with age.

Miriam pushes open the double doors, and my mouth drops open. The room is lined with bookshelves and rows of books. There are old dusty tomes and newer looking paperbacks. A ladder on rails slides along the back wall to reach the books on the upper level.

Comfy looking couches form a square in the center of the room, and off to one side is a nook with a sheepskin rug and a bean bag.

It's the type of library you could spend every rainy afternoon in for the rest of your life. You could live in here and never get through all the books.

Miriam's regarding me with a huge grin on her face.

"You are a reader then," she says knowingly. "I love seeing people's reaction when they come in here. If they're in awe, they're readers. If not, I take them down to the games room. But I think, Chantelle, you'll find something to keep you entertained here."

Her eyes twinkle when she speaks, but something she said bugs me.

"Do you show many people this room?"

Jealousy tugs at my chest. I wonder how many other women Alex has shown around here. I have no right to be jealous, but I can't stop the feeling. I want to be special to him, which is silly. I've only just met him, and he's only being kind because I'm hurt. But damn, I wish it was more than that.

Miriam gives me a knowing look as if she can read my thoughts.

"Not many, and no other women if that's what you're really asking."

I open my mouth to protest, but she waves her hand away. "Alex doesn't bring women here. The only guests he has are the Search and Rescue team. He's a private man, and you can understand why."

I frown at her.

"Why?"

She looks at me like I'm slow again. "Because of who he is."

I stare at her, trying to figure out what she's telling me. Am I supposed to recognize him?

"Who is he?"

She chuckles like I'm telling a joke, but when she sees my expression, her eyes widen. "Oh, you really don't know."

My mind's racing. What am I missing? If he's famous, I don't recognize him, but then I haven't had much time to follow the latest celebrity gossip.

"Should I?"

She chuckles her soft laugh again. "Maybe it's better if you don't know," she murmurs as she turns away. "He's a rich man who volunteers his time to Search and Rescue. That's all you need to know."

I want to ask more, but she's already at the door.

"I need to get my cookies out of the oven. I'll bring you one up with a cup of coffee for morning tea. Now choose a book and sit with that leg up, or we'll both be in trouble."

She's gone before I have time to ask any more questions. But as I brush my fingers along spines looking for the perfect read, my mind keeps going over the same problem.

Who the hell is Alex?

7

ALEX

The comms room hums with the sounds of computers and the quiet voice of Mateo on the phones. Most of the calls we get are people complaining about other campers or reports of bears which usually turn out to be racoons.

Suzie's on her tea break when I arrive, and I head to the staff kitchen to speak with her. She's in conversation with Erika, from the fire team. They're talking about some local dude who's returning from the military in a few weeks. A bit of a local hero, Suzie informs me. Suzie grew up around here and went to school with him.

Erika looks as unimpressed as I am.

"Nothing against the guy, but there are a lot of veterans on the mountain. They didn't all get a parade when they got back."

There's a parade happening in Hope for the guy, and I make a mental note to stay well away. I hate crowds, even ones to welcome heroes home.

"Any more news about the caller?" I ask Suzie.

She pours tea out of a silver pot through a strainer and into a small porcelain teacup before replacing the strainer on a special holder.

"We couldn't trace him if that's what you mean."

We record all calls, and if they're on long enough we get a good idea of where they're calling from. It helps track lost hikers who don't know where they are.

"How about the number he called from?"

Suzie raises her eyebrows at me. "Come on, Alex. You know I can't give you that information."

It's true she can't hand out information about callers, but if she looked the other way for a few minutes, it might give me enough time to get the info I need.

"Is that Earl Grey you're drinking?"

She nods, impressed that I remember. Suzie's a tea drinker, has been ever since she lived in England for three years, and her tea drinking rituals are cause for friendly banter, but today, they might be the break I need.

"Do you think you could make me one? The proper way?"

Suzie's eyes light up.

To a tea enthusiast, there's a proper way to brew it, with a correct water temperature and shit. She doesn't even take it with cream.

"Of course. You want one, Erika?"

The other woman screws her face up. "Nah, I'll stick to coffee."

Suzie flips the kettle to boil and takes down her tin of loose leaf Earl Grey.

"I'll just head to the bathroom," I say.

I leave her talking to Erika about the finer points of loose leaf over bagged tea. It'll keep her busy for at least another five minutes.

I feel kind of bad. I like Suzie. She's good at her job and an integral part of our team. But I need to know who Chantelle was hiking with and if they're a danger to her. And if she's not talking, then I'll find out myself.

When I get back to the comms room, Mateo is on a call and doesn't even glance my way as I lean over Suzie's computer and bring up the recording from yesterday. It doesn't take me long to pinpoint the phone tower it pinged off and the number. I write it down and hide the file.

I'll look the number up on my laptop as soon as I get the chance. I have ways of accessing networks that I don't want to do on Suzie's computer.

When I stroll into the kitchen, there's a steaming mug of what looks like brackish river water waiting for me.

"Thanks."

I take the mug and almost burn my tongue on the scalding liquid. Suzie beams at me and tells me about the cute little teashop in the village where she lived in England that was in a whitewashed cottage with a thatched roof.

I've heard the story before. But I smile politely and blow on the tea, taking another tentative sip and trying not to wince at the bitter flavor.

As soon as she leaves, I tip it down the sink.

"Sorry, Suzie."

I make a mental note to order her a box of Earl Grey loose leaf to make up for my waste.

After a quick visit to the Rangers' office to speak to Symon and the Sheriff, I park my Jeep down a secluded road and put my Starlink satellite on the roof. The internet springs to life, and I bounce it off a VPN before I enter the password to my secure network.

I take out the note with the number scribbled on it and then enter the code that gets me into the back end of where I shouldn't be.

Reams of data scroll down the screen, and I type in the number until I find what I'm looking for. Five minutes later, I've got the name of the person that phone number is registered to.

Chantelle Deeny.

The guy used her own phone to call her in.

I sit back, frustrated. I'm no closer to finding out who this asshole is.

8

ALEX

Thoughts of Chantelle pull me back to the cabin. I didn't like leaving her this morning, but I had to find out anything I could about her situation, which it turns out isn't much. She's as much a mystery to me as she was last night.

When I come in the cabin is quiet, and for a fearful moment I wonder if she tried to leave again. Not that I have any right to keep her here. It's for my own selfish reasons that I want her to myself.

The doctor said she needs bed rest, so at least I have that to back me up.

I find Chantelle in the library. She's fallen asleep with a Nora Roberts book open on her lap and her ankle propped up on the table.

Her lips have fallen open and her pink tongue

pokes out slightly, just like the little kitten she is. I stand for a while watching her, unable to take my eyes off of her. She looks so innocent and peaceful. The little worry lines that furrow her brow have vanished as she sleeps.

I grab a blanket from the back of an armchair and drape it over her.

She stirs, and her eyes flicker open. When they see mine, so close, she smiles.

"Where did you go?" she asks and then shuts her mouth quickly. "Sorry, it's none of my business."

I love it that she's interested, and I wonder if she missed me when she woke up.

"Why? Were you looking for me?"

She stretches in an adorable little kitten stretch.

"I must have fallen asleep."

"Good. You're meant to be resting."

Her nose wrinkles like she doesn't like being told what to do.

"When can I leave?"

Her words shouldn't hurt. Of course she wants to get back to her family, to her life. I just want more time to make her realize her life is here with me now.

"Anytime you like."

She raises her eyebrows like she doesn't believe me.

"So I can walk out of here anytime?"

I shake my head. "No, not on that ankle. It wouldn't be responsible for me to let you walk out of here. We're on the side of a mountain."

Her eyes bore into mine, and I wonder what's going on in her head. "So, I can't leave."

"You tell me where to drop you, and I'll take you there."

She looks away and folds her arms.

"The train station."

It's a start and the most she's opened up to me. I shouldn't be surprised that she took the train here. With what she was wearing on the hike, she's obviously a city girl.

"I can't let you get on a train with a sprained ankle, no phone, and no money. Tell me where to take you, and I'll drive you there."

So I can figure out what you're hiding, who the asshole was who left you, and find a way to make it all better.

She folds her arms and purses her lips together, saying nothing.

She's not going to talk. Whatever secret she's keeping, whoever she's protecting better be fucking worth it.

"I thought so."

She keeps her gaze on the window as I stand up. I'll

get no more out of Chantelle now. But I want to get to know my kitten while she's under my care.

"Rest up. Dinner is at six in the dining room."

I leave her to her book and head to my office.

9

CHANTELLE

The dining room is on the ground floor, and the table alone is bigger than the last room I called my own. French doors look out over the valley. The blood red sky tinges everything a pale rose and illuminates the dark shapes of the mountain peaks in the distance.

The air changes the moment Alex walks in the room. The skin on the back of my neck prickles, and heat surges through my body. His pine scent reaches me, and then I feel his hot breath tickle my neck.

"Beautiful, isn't it?"

I can't control the delicious shudder that trembles through my body. When I turn around Alex is behind me, a sardonic smile on his handsome face. He's wearing a dinner jacket over a pale blue shirt that hangs open at the collar. His dark denim jeans only make him look more handsome. Casually smart, not needing to impress anyone.

I swallow hard and look away, because he's too hard to look at. If I stare at him too long, I'll lose myself in him. I'll forget Chris and my real life, and that I can't do.

Alex holds out a glass of wine to me, and for a moment I'm tempted by the crimson liquid. How easy it would be to drink good wine with this man, get a buzz on, and forget my responsibilities? But I've seen where that can lead.

"No thank you." I shake my head. "I don't drink."

Surprise and curiosity cross his face before he moves to the bar in the corner of the room and opens a small fridge.

"I've got soda or juice."

I opt for an orange juice, and Alex surprises me by leaving both wine glasses aside and pouring himself a juice as well.

The table has been laid out for two. One place on the end and the other adjacent to it. I'm glad we aren't sitting at either end of the long table like some formal dinner. It feels cozy this way, intimate.

I use the crutches to get to the table, and Alex pulls the chair out for me.

A bread board is spread on the table with a selection of cured meats, homemade bread, and ramekins of oils and spreads that I don't know the names off.

I watch Alex take a slice of bread and dip it in the oil and I do the same, hoping he doesn't realize I don't know how the hell to eat this fancy food.

I have so many questions for him, so much I want to ask, but the one thing I really want to know is if he'll kiss me again.

"The clothes fit okay?" he asks.

I glance down at the floral blouse and flowing navy skirt I picked out for tonight. They fit perfectly. They're the nicest clothes I've ever owned.

"They're fine. I'll pay you back as soon as I can."

It will take me months of working to pay these off, but I don't want to tell him about my job stacking shelves at a department store. A job that I need to get back for in a few days. A job I can't afford to lose.

For a little while longer, I can play at this fantasy life, pretend I belong here in a mansion disguised as a cabin, with a handsome man who obviously has the money of a small nation.

He waves his hand dismissively. "Don't worry about it."

My lips press together. It's not wise to take gifts from strange men. They always want something from you.

But as I watch Alex sip his orange juice, I wonder if

it's okay if the thing they want is something you're willing to give.

"So what do you do?"

I jump in with a question before he does.

Alex spreads a gooey substance on the other half of his bread, and I do the same. It might be hummus, but I can't be sure.

He raises an eyebrow at me and there's a slight smile on his face, like there's a joke I'm missing.

"I'm in the tech business."

It's an evasive answer, and he doesn't expand on it. It makes me think of Miriam's comment that I should know who he is. He's got the looks of a movie star and the voice of a blues singer. But that doesn't fit with what he's just told me. I'm no closer to figuring out who the hell he is.

I take a bit of bread, and my taste buds tingle with sensation.

"Hmm, what is this?" I ask between mouthfuls, totally forgetting to play it cool.

Alex smiles. "Baba ganoush, made from eggplants. It's Miriam's own recipe."

"It's good."

"I'll pass on your compliments."

His eyes blaze into mine, and his hand lifts to my cheek. His thumb grazes the corner of my lips, and my breath hitches at the touch.

"You've got ganoush on your face."

Which is not a sentence I ever thought I'd hear.

I dart my tongue out to catch the stray food, but his thumb's still there and my tongue swipes against his skin.

Alex sucks in his breath, and his eyes grow dark.

I stare at him, both excited and terrified of the lust burning in his eyes that matches my own.

He leans forward, and his lips are inches from mine. I close my eyes, ready this time for his kiss.

The door swings open, and I spring away from Alex just as Miriam bustles into the room.

"Are you ready for your main course?" she asks.

I keep my eyes on the table even as I feel Alex's eyes on me. Another moment, and I would have been lost in his kiss.

Would that be so bad?

Miriam clears the board away and brings out two plates of poached fish. It's the best meal I've ever eaten, and I try not to scarf it down too fast.

We spend the rest of the evening talking about everything and nothing. I learn that Alex had this cabin built seven years ago when he moved here from Silicon Valley. That he loves solitude and is wary of people.

I'm still no closer to figuring out who he is or what he does.

But I'm just as evasive, so I can't complain. I give him half answers to his gentle prying. I tell him I have a younger brother and that our mother passed two years ago. That we're the only family left that each other has.

But I don't tell him the rest of it. I couldn't bear to see his lustful look turn to disgust. So we both stay silent on the real things while building our own best versions of ourselves.

I try to help clear the table, but Alex instructs me to sit.

He helps Miriam take the dishes back to the kitchen, and I hear them talking amiably and her low chuckle as they wash up together.

I sip hot chocolate and look out over the dark horizon. Glowing stars punctuate the sky where they peer out from the cloud cover that's rolled in.

Somewhere out there Chris is on his own, doing God knows what. With my belly full of food and my ankle resting on the coffee table as I look out over the star-laden sky, guilt gnaws at my stomach.

But I wouldn't be any good to him with my ankle sprained. If I went back now, no one would give me crutches. I'd be useless to him, and my recovery would take longer. If I can rest here for a few days longer, then I'll be stronger, physically and mentally. I'll be strong enough to look after him.

I'm not sure when I doze off, but I wake up as Alex lifts me into his arms.

It's becoming familiar, his carrying me like this, and I link my hands around the back of his neck and lean into his solid chest.

He carries me to my room, but as he sets me down on the bed I tug at his arms, pulling him down with me. I'm not sure what I want, but the pressure of his body on mine sends my pulse skittering.

"Chantelle…" he moans, and it comes out tortured.

He rolls onto the side, and he pulls me toward him. In the dim light, his eyes seem black.

"Kiss me."

I hate the pleading tone of my voice, but I need this from him. Before he finds out the truth, before he sends me away, I want the full fantasy. The mysterious man in my bed, to make me forget, to give me one good memory in my shitty life.

His lips find mine, his rough beard scratches my chin, and in the dark, he kisses me. The warmth spreads through my body, and I move underneath him.

His hands steal down my body, waking up every part of me. I've never been touched like this before, never been looked after. Which is how I feel as he gently runs his hand up my blouse and over my skin, exploring every part of me.

"You sure you're ready for this?"

His concern battles with his self-control, and I want his self-control to lose. I don't know who this man really is, but I want him to lose control with me.

"Yes."

He kisses me again, this time more urgent, hungry. His hand tugs at my bra, pulling the cup down so his thumb can strum my nipple. My back aches at his touch, and my hips press against his hardness. I gasp at the solidness, of what it means.

I've never done this before, but it feels so right. Tonight, I'm not thinking about anyone else. I'm letting my instincts guide me.

There's a vibration and the sound of his phone ringing.

Alex keeps kissing me, trying to ignore it. The phone stops only to start up again immediately.

"Fuck." He sits back on his haunches. "It might be the rescue team."

He pulls his phone out of his pocket as I try not to show my disappointment.

"What," he barks down the line.

It makes me giggle. I'd hate to be on the receiving end of that call. I hope it's not the rescue people. They all seemed so nice.

Alex runs a hand through his hair as he listens to the call.

"I'll call you back." He shuffles off the bed, and I hate how disappointed I feel.

Alex stands at the end of the bed, and I suddenly feel exposed. Exposed and stupid with my blouse half open and my lips swollen from his kisses.

He eyes me with regret and something else: resolve.

"I shouldn't have done that. You're here to heal. I shouldn't have taken advantage of you."

The words sting. It hurts that he regrets kissing me, because there's nothing in the last five minutes that I regret apart from the fact it didn't go further.

I pull my blouse together and sit up. I won't let him see me vulnerable. I won't let him see that side of me.

"I asked you to kiss me, remember." I try to make light of it, but my voice sounds shriller than I wanted.

He runs a hand through his hair.

"I have to deal with a work issue. You need to get some sleep and rest. I'll see you in the morning."

With that he closes the door, and I'm left feeling exposed and vulnerable and wondering what the hell just happened.

ALEX

My cock's painfully hard, and leaving Chantelle on the bed, ready and willing is probably the hardest thing I've ever had to do. But Calvin's words ring in my ear.

Don't take advantage of her.

Chantelle's injured and vulnerable, and there's still a hell of a lot she's not telling me. Having sex with her now would definitely be taking advantage.

It was lucky I got a call from Aaron, or who knows what would have happened.

My cock twitches painfully. He knows exactly what would have happened, and he's not forgiving me for it.

I retreat down the hall to my office before I change my mind and go in there and claim Chantelle the way I've been aching to ever since I laid eyes on her.

As soon as I get in my office, I lean on the door and pull my dripping cock out of my pants. It only takes a few tugs and the memory of her body pressed against mine until I release into my hand.

But it's unsatisfying. My heart knows it, and my cock knows it.

Chantelle's no less of a mystery to me than she was when I first brought her in. She opened up about her family, telling me childhood stories with a wistful expression on her face, her and her brother getting up to mischief unchecked because her mother was never around.

It was what she left unsaid that filled in the blanks for me. Her mother working hard to provide for her kids, no mention of a father. The affection she feels for her little brother.

Then she told me about her mother's illness. How she nursed her through it and looked after her brother. Seventeen years old with more responsibilities than most adults.

But all her stories were from the past. She was evasive about the present and changed the subject when I asked about her brother now. My mind's running away with possibilities. Was it her brother who left her on the mountain? And why would someone do that when by all accounts she's been taking care of him for the last few years?

I was just as evasive. Chantelle must be the only woman on the mountain who doesn't know who I am. It's refreshing.

I don't have many friends here, aside from the rescue crew, but they're better friends than anyone from my old life.

My phone rings again, and I answer it to an impatient Aaron.

Putting thoughts of Chantelle aside, I fire up my laptop. I may have officially retired seven years ago, but I stayed on in the company as a silent partner, available to consult whenever needed.

Aaron explains the problem, and I spend the next few hours talking through the options.

He knows what he's doing. These days I'm more of a sounding board, and I wonder if the time's come to step back completely. To sell my remaining shares in the company and fully retire. Perhaps it's time for a new phase of my life.

A phase where Chantelle and our children become the center of my world, where my only job is to keep them happy and fed and secure.

11

CHANTELLE

I wake up with a dull ache between my legs that's grounded in need, different from the ache in my ankle.

Frustration makes me grumpy when Miriam comes in to bring me breakfast. She's not Alex, and he's the one I want to see, the one I want answers from. Like who the fuck is he and why did he leave me last night when we were so close to doing something I definitely wouldn't regret?

He's got me wound up so tight I feel delirious. This place is making me forget who I am or why I'm here, and *I like it.*

But it's not Miriam's fault. I sit up when she pulls the curtain back, swallowing down my frustration. I'm torn between wanting to get out of here and wanting to find Alex and rip his damn clothes off.

I swing my legs out of bed, and sharp pain travels up my leg.

Miriam raises her eyebrows at me.

"Another day of rest, my dear, and you should be walking again. But if you overdo it too soon…" she shakes her head and tuts at me. "You'll be here for another week."

She bustles out of the room, and I'm left with a plate of honey-coated waffles wondering if that would be so bad.

But it would. Chris is out there probably forgetting to eat, while I'm here getting waited on and living like a princess.

I must leave today.

But when I put pressure on my ankle, I know there's no way I'm walking out of here on my own. Which only leaves getting a lift from Alex.

I chew on a piece of my hair, turning over the consequences. I could ask him to drop me in the middle of Charlotte. It's where I'd begin my search for Chris. But he'd only ask questions. I get the feeling that unless I give him an address, he won't take me anywhere.

Of course, I could go to the authorities. But I'm even less eager to explain my situation to the police, and they won't let me evade any questions.

As I eat my waffles, I contemplate this strange

prison I find myself in. I'm being looked after, fed, and kissed by a hot stranger. Most women wouldn't want to leave, but most women don't have a brother who's counting on them, no matter how shitty he is to them.

Because no matter how hard I want Alex, no matter how well I feel looked after, the fact remains. Chris is my responsibility, and I must do whatever it takes to look after him.

I'm in a position of privilege here in this mansion/cabin. There must be something I can do while I'm here to make things easier for myself and Chris.

The answer when it comes makes my skin crawl. But if it's what I need to do to help my brother, then it's what I'll do.

It's time to explore the cabin and find out exactly who Alex is.

After breakfast, I insist on washing myself. I need to get my independence back, and that starts with looking after my own shower.

With a fresh pair of yoga pants and a t-shirt with a wolf printed on it, I hobble to the library.

Miriam brings me a cup of herbal tea and makes sure I'm settled before leaving me alone.

As soon as she's gone, I hobble to the door and peer into the hallway, listening.

There are no sounds of voices, nothing to tell me where Alex is. I limp across the hall and start with the first door I come across.

The first thing I notice is the wide screen. It takes up almost an entire wall. A comfy couch is in front of it with armchairs on either side. Speakers surround the room, and a gaming console and controller sit on the entertainment unit under the wide screen.

I imagine Alex in here, on his own, playing games on the PlayStation, or maybe he watches movies. I wonder what he's into. War movies full of action is my guess.

An image pops into my mind of how easy it would be to spend nights in this room, watching Netflix together or gaming. I haven't gamed since we got evicted from Mom's old place. We had to sell Chris's console, and I promised I'd buy him a new one as soon as we got back on our feet. Another promise I haven't kept.

I close the door on the entertainment room before the guilt claws at my stomach.

I hobble to the next room, and this one's got a fireplace and another couch and more comfy armchairs. For a man who claims to be a recluse, there are a lot of seats in this cabin.

This room feels more intimate, and I step inside and close the door behind me.

There's a framed photo on the wall of a much younger Alex with no lines on his closely shaved face. With no beard or silver flecks in his hair, he looks at least a decade younger. He's wearing a dinner suit and smiling as he holds up an award, the center of a group of people. I squint to read the small lettering engraved on the fiberglass plaque. "Start-up of the year, 2011."

He's holding his thumb over the name of the company so I can't see it, but a tingle goes down my spine.

He said he escaped Silicon Valley, and I guessed he was a programmer or something. But judging by the way he's front and center in the photo holding the award up, it looks like he ran a company.

There's a writing desk in the corner of the room, and I pull open the small drawer to the side. Inside is a stack of old magazines. I pull them out and flick through the covers. Photos of celebrity couples and click bait headlines scream at me, and I wonder what the hell he's got tabloid magazines for.

A pang of jealousy pierces my chest. What if they belong to another woman?

But I've seen no evidence of another woman anywhere else in the cabin aside from Miriam.

I flick through the magazines, and the cover of one

catches my eye. It's Alex, smiling at the camera and clutching the hand of a beautiful blonde woman whose made up face looks vaguely familiar.

The dream couple, or another casualty of the Playboy of the Valley?

My mouth drops open. Are they talking about Alex? Is he the Playboy of the Valley they're referring to?

I flick through the magazine until I get to the story. It's a filler piece speculating on his relationship with the woman who I learn is an actress from a popular daytime soap.

My heart's racing even though this happened over ten years ago. I'm jealous of this woman, that she had something with Alex, even though I've got no right to be jealous.

I close the magazine and pick up another one. In this one he's with a different woman, a model from South Korea. There's the same speculation, the same catty remarks and implications about the woman and her morals, which makes me angry. Alex is the town playboy, but anyone he dates has loose morals.

I'm angry on behalf of those women, even as jealousy stings my heart.

In the next picture he looks wary, no longer smiling. The headline screams about his latest break up.

On the final magazine cover, he has his hand up in front of his face, a scowl the only part of him you can see as he walks past the camera.

I let the magazine fall onto the pile on my lap. It all makes sense. He's some kind of tech guy celebrity who the paparazzi chewed up and spat out. He came here to escape, to get away from it all. To get away from all those beautiful women.

That last part doesn't make sense.

Why is he attracted to me if he could have his pick of A-list celebrities? Is it because there's no one on the mountain who's up to his usual standard? Am I the only one gullible enough now to fall for his easy charm?

I've been stupid to think he could possibly feel something for an overweight nobody. It's painfully clear I have to get out of here now. I have to leave Alex to the kind of woman he's used to and get back to Chris where I belong. It's been a nice fantasy for a few days, but it's time to get back to my people.

I put the magazines back in the drawer.

On the shelf next to the desk, there's the award that was in the photo. I read the name of the company, and my mouth drops open.

It's a social media platform that I use every day. That thousands, no millions of people use every day.

My eyes scan the shelf, and it's full of awards for the same company.

Then it hits me.

Alex is Alexander Young, the founder of one of the biggest social platforms of the last decade. No wonder he has his pick of women. No wonder he built a mansion/cabin on the side of a mountain. Hell, he's probably rich enough to own the mountain. I am way out of my depth here.

I need to go, and I need to go now.

I turn to get my crutches where I left them propped against the couch, and that's when I notice the miniature gold statue.

It's on a shelf next to the awards and I pick it up cautiously, feeling the weight of it. There's no writing on it. It's not an award, just a pure gold ornament. A miniature owl, the kind of random thing a rich person would have in their mansion. It's heavy in my hands, pure gold. I've pawned enough of it in my time to know it by weight.

It would keep me and Chris safe for a few weeks, months maybe if he stays out of trouble. Then, with my job, it might be enough for a deposit on an apartment. Somewhere we can move into, get away from the people who drag him down.

This golden owl could be the start of a new life.

But can I take it from the man who's taken me in, looked after me, fed me, and bought me clothes?

He's also the man who kissed me, who would have taken advantage of me because that's what privileged people do.

But not Alex, my mind screams.

He volunteers for Search and Rescue. He's not a bad man.

I shake the doubt from my mind. What do I know about the Playboy of the Valley? Nothing. And he won't even miss the tiny owl among all his wealth.

With the owl heavy in my pocket, I slip out of the room. And straight into the arms of Alexander Young.

I gasp in surprise, and my crutches clatter to the floor as I almost topple over, but he's there to catch me. My arms instinctually clutch his and I lean against his chest, breathing in his woodsy masculine scent. Despite knowing who he is and what I have to do, my knees go weak and my core pulls up tight.

"Why aren't you resting?"

His concern seems genuine, and I almost pull the owl out of my pocket and hand it over. But he's from a different world than I am. I can't be sure of anything he says.

"I got bored," I lie. "I'm not used to being cooped up."

"Hmmm." His steel eyes bore into mine, but he doesn't let me go.

"I've got a remedy for boredom."

His voice is gravelly, and I think he's going to kiss me again, but instead he tips me upright and retrieves my crutches from where they clattered to the floor.

He leads me to the room I explored earlier, the entertainment room, and turns on the PlayStation.

"Do you like games, Chantelle?"

He's got a smile on his lips, and I don't know if it's a loaded question. I'm way out of my depth with him and not sure if the entire last few days have been a game. I'm up against the Playboy of the Valley. I don't stand a chance.

"I used to play FIFA with my brother."

He passes me a controller and surprises me by sitting next to me on the sofa. He hitches up his grey sweatpants and takes off his sweater, revealing a tight t-shirt underneath.

I can't marry up the casual, relaxed man next to me with the playboy billionaire in the magazines.

"Which country do you want to be?"

"Brazil." I always played Brazil.

Before I have time to question what I'm doing, the game's on and my fingers are working overtime to dribble and kick and score. It must be muscle memory from all those wasted evenings keeping

Chris company and out of trouble. Because no matter who the hell Alex is, mountain man rescuer or playboy billionaire, I'm not going to let him beat me at FIFA.

Miriam brings us sandwiches for lunch and a pitcher of juice. And at some point, between tournaments, the light fades into dusk.

When she brings in two bowls of pasta for dinner, I stretch and blink as if seeing my surroundings for the first time. I'm surprised to find myself still in the massive mansion/cabin, joking casually with a tech celebrity.

Because as the day has gone on, what I've found out about Alex seems to matter less and less. We've laughed and joked, and for the first time in a long time, I've had fun.

I finger the owl in my pocket, torn between revealing it to him or quietly putting it back. I'm drawn to him, and I don't know if it's real of if it's his natural charm with women.

All I know is once the dinner's been cleared away and we're sitting on the couch nursing hot chocolates, and another day has gone by and I'm still here, it feels right, even at the same time as the guilt weighs me down.

"Your dressing needs changing."

I glance at my ankle and the bandage is hanging

half off, and it's dirty from where I've been dragging it around.

"Come on."

We go into my room where a stack of bandages has been left, and I sit on the bed while Alex kneels before me with my foot propped on his knee.

Shivers go through my body as he unwraps the bandage, holding my foot up to carefully inspect it.

"It's healing," he says. "The swelling's gone down. You'll be able to start putting pressure on it tomorrow."

He rubs arnica cream into the ankle, and every touch is like a mini firework going off in my body.

He tucks the bandage in on itself, but he doesn't drop my foot. His careful fingers move slowly up my calf, causing tendrils of heat to snake up my thighs and between my legs.

I'm instantly wet with need. I long to have his hands on me, his lips on me. My mind is reeling trying to figure out which man Alex is: the playboy I read about in the magazines or the caring man before me, wrapping a strange girl's ankle in a clean bandage.

Our eyes meet, and in this moment, I don't care who he is. I just want him to kiss me again. As if sensing my need, his hands slide up my legs and his lips press to the skin of my calf, just above the bandage.

"I've been thinking about kissing you all day," he murmurs, and a shiver courses through me.

His lips move up my legs as his hands pull my hips toward him. I should resist. I should fight the playboy, but I'm powerless. My body wants this. It wants him. I've never been with a man before. I've been too busy surviving. But with this man, I want to give him everything. Even if it is only for one night.

He pulls me toward him and kisses my lips, a slow, deep kiss, and if I didn't know better, I'd think it was a kiss full of promises. But I know what he is: a playboy. He's seduced hundreds of women; I have to remember that.

"I've wanted you since I first saw you," Alex murmurs. "It's crazy, Chantelle. I've only known you a few days, but it feels like forever."

His kisses move down my neck, causing new fireworks with every soft brush of his lips, with every whisper of warm breath. The words are as hypnotic as his kisses, drawing me to him.

"You're mine, Chantelle. Say you'll be mine."

A moan escapes my lips. I long to belong to him. But he means for this night only. I'll play along. I'll let him seduce me, and tomorrow I'll deal with the consequences.

"I'm yours."

He groans at my words, and my heart squeezes. I

wish it was forever he was promising me. I wish he meant I could be his forever. But I'm so desperate with my need to belong that I'll take whatever I can get, whatever he can give me.

"I'm a virgin, Alex."

He gives a sharp intake of breath. "Oh kitten."

"I want you to be my first."

Because I do. What better man to give myself to than the stranger who rescued me and took me in and gave me two days of care. It hardly makes up for a lifetime without, but I'll take what I can get.

"I'll take care of you, Chantelle. Now and forever."

He mumbles more pretty words full of promises that he'll never keep.

This must be what it's like to be seduced by a playboy. I'm fascinated and turned on and heartbroken all at once. Because I don't care who he is or what he's done before. I wish this was real. I've fallen for my mountain man rescuer.

His hands work at my yoga pants, lifting the hem up and tugging at my panties. His lips move back down my body, trailing kisses over my now exposed skin.

There's a moment of panic as he peels my top off, exposing my flabby bits, so much more flesh than the tiny actresses and models he was photographed with.

But he kisses every part of me, his hands moving

over my skin as if he doesn't care about a bit of extra weight.

It makes me bolder, and when his head dips between my legs, when his kisses trail up my inner thigh, I open my thighs. I open them wide and let him in.

12
ALEX

Chantelle tastes of the earth and sweetness and all things good and pure. She's the antithesis of any woman I've ever been with before, more real and substantial than some model looking for a billionaire to latch onto. The fact that she's unaware of who I am makes this all the more real.

I lick her up, taking my time with her virgin pussy. Slowing inserting a finger, and then two as I lap at her delicious flower.

Her juices flow over my chin, coating my beard and filling my nostrils with the scent of her.

I give her everything I've got. She's my future, my woman. I don't know what she's hiding, but I'll take it on.

A search on her has come to a dead end. She went quiet on social media after her mother died. I could use other means to find her secrets, but I stopped myself at casual social stalking. I'll let her open up to me in her own time, and when she does, I'll use all my resources to help her with whatever she needs.

It doesn't take long for Chantelle to come undone on my tongue. I clamp my mouth to her sweet bud until she stops trembling. Then I climb up on the bed next to her.

She's breathing hard, and the moonlight streams in the window onto her hair fanned out around her face.

"You're beautiful," I murmur, twisting a strand in my fingers.

I want to claim her tonight, but I'm wary of her ankle. I thought having a taste would be enough, but it's not. I'll never get enough of this woman.

Her hands slide over my chest and down to my belt.

"Are you sure?" If she's not ready, I won't push. It'll kill me, but I won't push her.

"I want you, Alex."

My heart sings at her words. "I want you too, kitten. I want you in my bed every night for the rest of our lives."

She gives me a funny look like she doesn't believe me, and I'm probably coming on too strong. But I can't keep what I'm feeling hidden any longer. She doesn't have to believe me yet.

I've got my entire life to convince Chantelle of what I've known since I first laid eyes on her. Chantelle's mine. She's my woman, my soul mate. The only woman I'll ever want.

I kiss her again, putting all my unexpressed feelings into that kiss. Letting her know with my body how much she means to me.

Her pussy's slick with need as I slide my fingers between her folds, working her into a frenzy until she's coming again. Trembling on my palm with the most beautiful little moans I ever heard.

As she comes undone, I slide my fingers out and slide the tip of my cock in. She gasps, and her pussy clenches around me. I almost lose control, but I grab her hips and hold her in place.

"You move again, and I'll come."

She giggles. "Isn't that the idea?"

"Not until I've made you orgasm at least another two times."

Her eyes go wide, and I use the moment to push in further.

She winces as I push through her virgin barrier.

"Alex!"

She clings onto my shoulder, and I hold her in place.

"Breathe angel. Just breathe."

We rock gently until her sweet pussy gets used to

the intrusion of my cock. It doesn't take long until she's rocking her hips, pulling me toward her and wanting more.

I control the pace, wary of her sore ankle and her tender pussy. But she's so God damn tight, it's hard not to let go. Especially when she wraps her legs around me and cries out, my name echoing into the darkness and wakening something deep inside me. A possessiveness I've never felt before.

I've been with women who wanted me for my money, women who wanted me for my fame, but never a woman as sweet as this who just wants to be with me for me.

As she clings onto me, her body shuddering, I let myself go. Thinking about our future together. About getting her pregnant and keeping her here always in my cabin.

Afterwards we lie together, her back fitted snugly against my front and my arms wrapped protectively around her.

I've claimed her now, my kitten. She's mine, and there's nothing in this world that will keep us apart.

Chantelle's breathing deepens, but I stay awake for a long time listening to her sleep. For the first time someone is with me for me, and it fills me with a warm contentment.

In the morning, I'll call Aaron and pull out of the

business completely. I'll make Chantelle tell me what the hell's going on so I can fix it. Then I'll take her to a chapel with only my rescue team at the ceremony and marry her before anyone from my past life can get a hold of her.

And then I'll tell her who I am.

I've hidden away on the mountain for too long. But with Chantelle by my side, I'm done hiding. I've got privilege and more money than I can handle. I've been thinking about starting some kind of charity project for a long time. I've always donated to causes, but it's time I set one up for myself. And with Chantelle by my side, I can do anything.

13

CHANTELLE

I wake up with a warm body pressed against my back and a contented feeling that's eluded me since before Mom got sick. Sunlight streams through the window, and I lie for a moment enjoying the sound of Alex's rhythmic breathing behind me.

My body aches in new ways from all the things we did last night. We woke in the night to have sex again, clinging onto each other, and in the darkness of the night, I could almost believe it meant something. But I know better than that.

Through a crack in the curtains the mountains are in view, solid and peaceful. The same way that Alex's body feels against mine.

I lie a few moments longer, enjoying the peace for as long as I can. Wondering what it would be like to wake up every morning with a warm body by your side, feeling safe and secure.

And loved.

Love. I push the thought out of my head even as my heart whispers the truth of it. I've being falling for Alex in the few days I've been here. How could I not? But I'm under no illusion about the way he feels about me. I've seen the magazines. He's a playboy. This is what he does. Seduces women.

I let myself be seduced, and I don't regret a thing. But sometime today, I've got to get back to reality.

Alex stirs beside me, and I roll over in bed to look at him.

With mussed up hair and sleep in his eyes, he's even more handsome than ever.

I could get used to this. Waking up next to him every morning.

Of course I could. If only I had the chance.

Alex's eyes flutter open, and he smiles when he sees me watching him. My heart squeezes. I wish it was a genuine smile for me. But I know better than to be fooled by his charm.

"Hey, beautiful."

My damn heart flutters at his words. The longer I stay, the more danger I am of falling in love with this man. Who am I kidding? I'm already in love with him.

I sit up in bed, pulling the sheets up with me,

suddenly feeling shy about my exposed body, sure he can read my emotions all over it. Alex traces a fingertip down my arm, and I shiver despite myself. His touch is enough to set my heart racing.

"You want some breakfast?"

He rolls out of bed and tugs on his clothes. "It's Miriam's day off, but I make a mean omelet."

I watch him dress, the lean muscles in his torso rippling as he bends down to retrieve his sweatpants.

Regret tugs at my heart, regret that this can only be a one-time thing. Heat burns at the corners of my eyes, and I look away quickly.

I will not cry in front of this man. I will not be the discarded one night stand.

Sticking my chin out, I climb out of bed and only wince slightly when my ankle hits the floor. The swelling's gone down, and I can put pressure on it without it hurting so much.

"I'm going to take a shower."

I hate the idea of washing his scent off me, but it might be the last opportunity I have for a hot shower for a while, so I'm going to take it.

Alex lets out a strangled groan. "I would join you, but I don't think your ankle could take it." He kisses the top of my head. "Another time."

"Another time," I echo, plastering a smile on my face, as if there's going to be another time. As if the

Playboy of the Valley wants another time with a girl like me.

I hate myself for having these thoughts, so I quickly head to the bathroom and crank the shower up to scalding.

As steam fills the room, I let out a deep breath.

I just had the best night of my life with a man who will never be mine. And it *hurts*. My chest feels like it's going to crack right open with the pressure. But I won't show him my pain. I won't be one of those girls begging for more of his affection.

I take my time in the shower, doing a full hair wash and scrubbing every part of me. When I get out, my skin is pink and my fingertips puckered.

I pull on the yoga pants I had on yesterday and choose a simple t-shirt from the rack. Something that won't look out of place in my regular life. My hand slides into the pocket and clasps the golden owl.

Thinking about what this owl will mean for me and Chris, the guilt for my brother dissipates a little only to be replaced by a different kind of guilt. I'm stealing from Alex, the guy who rescued me and looked after me.

I should put it back. Chris and I will cope. We've done it before.

I pull the owl out of my pocket and hold it up to the mirror. I should leave it on the bathroom counter.

The gold shimmers in the bathroom light and makes me think of the new start this could give us. I could get Chris the help he needs, get us a place to live, maybe even start the psychology degree I've been wanting to do.

I slip the owl back into my pocket and head to the kitchen.

Alex is singing along to a Taylor Swift song, a dishcloth thrown over his shoulder as he moves egg around in a pan. The smell of bacon makes my mouth water, and I perch on one of the kitchen counter stools.

"What do you want to do today? More FIFA?"

I have to tell Alex that I need to get home, but if I do there's a chance he'll convince me to stay longer, and I don't need much convincing. I hate myself for being so weak around him. I need to get back to Chris.

Alex sets a plate of food down in front of me and slides onto a stool. I'm about to open my mouth to tell him when his phone rings.

Alex holds a finger up to me. "Hold that thought, kitten." He frowns at the number on his phone. "It's Search and Rescue."

I nibble on a piece of bacon while he takes the call. He turns the speaker off, and his frown deepens as he listens to the person on the other end of the line. When he hangs up the phone, his expression is dark.

"There's been an avalanche up the mountain."

My hand flies to my mouth, "Oh my God. Is everyone okay?"

"It was early, before the ski hills were open, but some staff were up that way. Luckily, it's the end of the season and some of the runs are already closed. We don't know if anyone's missing yet, but I need to be there in case."

He's already reaching for his keys, breakfast forgotten.

"Of course."

It's what he does. Alex helps people who need him.

"Help yourself to anything in the kitchen and rest that ankle. I'll be back as soon as I can."

He kisses me on the forehead, then takes my cheeks in his hands and gives me a long, slow kiss that I feel all the way to my core.

This kiss feels like love. It feels like a promise. But it can't be. I'm an inexperienced girl who has no idea how a playboy like Alex works. He must have kissed a hundred women this way.

"And don't go anywhere."

He smiles, and I give him a smile back. My gaze runs over his face, trying to commit every detail to memory. The tiny scar on his throat, the lines around his eyes, the flecks of silver in his beard, the scent of pines and expensive cologne.

I want to tell him not to go, that I love him, that I need him, but I've only known him a few days. It even sounds crazy to me.

"Be careful." My voice comes out as a squeak.

"I will."

And then he's gone. Out the back corridor to the garage. I hear the door creaking open and the engine of his Jeep starting.

I hobble to the window to watch as the Jeep pulls out of the garage. The gate slides silently open and Alex drives off up the mountain road, kicking up dust behind him.

"Goodbye."

My voice is swallowed by the silence of the empty cabin.

14
ALEX

The sun's high in the sky when I drive through the gates and back to the cabin. It was a hard few hours, searching the snow with special dogs and equipment until we heard that everyone was accounted for.

The Lodge put out a free hot meal for the rescue team, but I was in too much of a hurry to get back to Chantelle.

Thoughts of her fill my mind as I hit the button that opens the gate to my property. Last night was the best night of my life, claiming my woman, but I felt she was holding back. Maybe it's all been too fast for her. Or maybe it's whatever secret she's hiding.

I'm going to speak to her today, tell her how I feel, and hopefully she'll feel safe enough to open up, to tell me what's going on so I can fix it for her. This woman's my life, my future, and she needs to know that.

My attention is caught by the side gate swinging open in the breeze. It's the small gate that lets people through without having to open the main gate for vehicles. Unease stirs in the pit of my stomach. Maybe Miriam stopped by and left it open.

I drive through the gate and hit the brakes. The garage door is wide open. Did I leave it open in my haste to leave? I can't be sure. The uneasy feeling intensifies as I park the Jeep.

"Chantelle!" I call as soon as I get out of the Jeep, even though she could be anywhere in the cabin.

I move quickly to the stairs but pull up short when I notice the empty space where my scooter is usually parked. It's vintage, useless on a mountain, but I love the old scooter and haven't had the heart to part with it. I leant it to Miriam for a while for her boys to get around town.

"Shit."

The scooter's gone, and it's small enough to fit through the side gate. I race upstairs calling for Chantelle, but the silence already tells me what I'm going to find.

The cabin is empty.

"Fuck."

The unease is a heavy weight in my stomach that

churns and tosses until I think I'm going to throw up. After what we did last night, I can't believe she'd just leave.

Then I see the note in a neat script written on the back of a letter.

Thanks for looking after me, but I need to get back to help my brother.

I'll never forget my night with the Playboy of the Valley.
Chantelle

"Fuck."

Chantelle knew who I was all along. And just like every other woman I've met, she only wanted me because of some goddam label a shitty journalist put on me to sell a few magazines.

I thought Chantelle didn't know me. She's younger than me by at least ten years, and I'm guessing she hasn't had much time to keep up with the trashy magazines that plastered my face all over them every time I went on a date. Labelled Silicon Valley's most eligible bachelor or biggest heartbreaker depending on the mood of the day. Eventually just the Playboy of the Valley, a name that followed me around attracting even more women who thought they'd be the one to tame me. Not that I need taming. The magazines exaggerated my life. They made me into a caricature. The magazines will construct their own narrative about someone if it sells more copies. But the reputation stuck.

It's what drove me here to the mountain, to grow my beard long and hide away. Occasionally a tabloid will run a feature speculating on where I am. I've deliberately left a false trail; I have people who let rumors slip. I was spotted in Paris for New Year's Eve, in Milan during fashion week, at a Buddhist temple in Tibet.

But the truth is I've been here all along, hiding in plain sight on the side of a mountain where people care more about how kind and genuine you are than the numbers in your bank account.

I thought Chantelle was one of those people. I got complacent.

My chest feels like it's been squeezed, and I grope around wildly for the kitchen counter wondering if I'm having a fucking heart attack.

The woman I thought was mine was just like all the rest. The sweet, innocent woman with kitten eyes and secrets only wanted me for one thing.

How could I get it so wrong?

Or maybe I didn't?

I think about Chantelle falling asleep reading a

book, laughing as she kicked my ass at FIFA, eating bread and pasta with a healthy appetite and no mention of carbs. So different from any woman I've ever dated. Chantelle, the reluctant patient who just wanted to get back to her brother. I *know* her, and she is different.

It's stupid. It's only been two days, but she's not like all the rest. She's different, genuine. I'm sure she is.

I need to find her.

Grabbing my keys, I race back to the Jeep.

Forty minutes later, I pull up out in front of the Hope Train station. She mentioned coming here by train, and my guess that she's come here is correct. My scooter is parked in the motorbike area with the helmet resting on the seat. I pick it up, and the keys are underneath. She must have known I'd look for her here.

I touch the engine, but it's stone cold.

There are no trains at the station, and I jog down the length of both platforms but she's not there.

The man at the ticket office gives me a list of every train that's left in the last six hours. She could have been on any one of them, and they might not have even been her final destination.

If she left the cabin straight after I did, she could be miles away by now.

One thing's for sure. I'm not going to let her get away without talking to her.

I glance at the list of trains and their destinations. Hope is too small a station to have CCTV, but most of the other stations do. It'll take time, but it's time to call on my networks to find my girl.

15

CHANTELLE

Two weeks later…

A dull throb vibrates through my ankle as I tiptoe over the debris strewn across the floor to get to the only window in the room. After two weeks the ankle's almost healed, but I didn't sleep last night and it's too dark to see what's on the floor, so my contorted walk, trying to dodge passed out bodies and plastic bags of belongings, is making it ache.

But a sore ankle is the least of my concerns.

The air is thick with coils of cigarette smoke and the stench of too many unwashed human bodies. Perspiration makes the t-shirt stick to my back, and it's with relief that I reach the window.

The latch catches and won't budge, too blocked

with rust and mold and some grey gunk that I try not to touch.

Chris groans, and I make my way back to the stained mattress he's lying on. His eyes are glazed, and there's a smile on his face.

My heart squeezes every time I see that smile. The smile that used to come freely as a boy and now only appears when he's high.

It took me two days to find him when I got back from the mountain. He was living under an overpass, the money that he got from selling my phone and other meagre belongings already used up.

When I took Chris walking in the mountains, he had been clean for two weeks. Getting back to nature is supposed to help recovering addicts, and I stupidly thought a hike in the mountains would do him good. I thought it would give him a natural high, release endorphins. Turns out he was just waiting for an opportunity to jump me. To mug his own sister.

The sprained ankle wasn't entirely his fault. I did that as I lunged after him, scraping my arm and knees as I went down.

Some people would say I'm foolish to forgive him. That mugging his own sister is going too far, and you can't help those who don't want to be helped. I've heard it all before.

But Chris is my brother, and he's the only family I

have left. My little brother who mom left me responsible for. My little brother who I've utterly failed.

He giggles and reaches into the air, grasping at something I can't see.

My shift at the department store starts in an hour, and I'll have to leave him here. It's an abandoned house that junkies have taken over. At least it has mattresses and is sheltered, better than an underpass.

My fingers run over the lump where the golden owl is hidden by my hip. I haven't been able to bring myself to pawn it yet, which is stupid. I could get a deposit on an apartment with that money for the both of us.

Chris is registered for state rehab again. He's done the first stage before, but the second stage is oversubscribed, and there's always a wait. He's never made it to the second tier.

He was only thirteen when mom got sick and seventeen when she died. I tried to be a mother to him, but it wasn't enough.

Chris has undiagnosed ADHD, and the turmoil of his world being turned upside down was something he couldn't cope with. If he could get clean, there's no reason why he couldn't hold down a job, meet a girl, have a normal life. All the things I want for him. But the longer he uses, the harder it is to see a life that's anything else but these endless cycles of rehab and using and rehab and using.

I glimpsed another life once. For two days, I was someone else.

I was loved.

My heart clenches when I think of Alex.

I bury the thought of him deep. There's no point pining over some rich dude that I'll never have a chance with. If he ever saw me in a place like this, if he knew I slept in a woman's shelter and my brother was a junkie, he would have run a mile.

There's the sound of shuffling feet by the door and I look up, always on guard. I keep the owl in a pouch taped to my hip. When you've been on this trip long enough, you get to learn all the tricks.

A man stands by the door, and my breath hitches. It's dark in here, and in the dim light he looks like Alex.

"Chantelle."

My heart misses a beat. It's him. It's Alex. The Playboy of the Valley in the most squalid part of Charlotte.

Except he's not the Playboy anymore. He's a kind man who volunteers his time to rescue people and took me in to make sure I healed properly.

"What are you doing here?"

He doesn't even flinch as he walks over, stepping

around a man passed out on a mattress. The closer he gets, the less air I have to breath, until he's taking up all my space. His scent fills my nostrils, my skin prickles, and all my senses spring to life.

"This is Chris?"

He indicates my brother who has a glazed, faraway look in his eye.

"How do you know about Chris?"

I clutch my chest, trying to still my heart. I never told him any of this, because how could I tell the man in the mansion about my shitty existence? About the poverty and waste of life that I see every day.

"I had to find you."

Realization hits. He's not here for me. He's here for the owl. He noticed it was missing and realized I stole it.

I swallow the disappointment and reach into my yoga pants, the same ones he bought me, to retrieve it from its hiding place.

Alex frowns as my hands slip into my waist band.

"What are you…?"

He stops short when I pull out the owl. "Here you go. Sorry I took it. I was desperate."

I hold it out to him, but he doesn't take it. I glance around to check if he's been filming this or anything.

"Are you going to prosecute me?" The last thing I

need is to get in trouble with the law. Who would look after Chris then?

"What? Of course not."

"Then why are you here?"

He frowns at me and takes a step closer, making it hard to breathe.

"I'm here for you."

My pulse quickens at his words, but that's all they are. Words.

"Why didn't you tell me?" His gaze flicks to Chris and to the room in general. The squalor, the brown stain on the ceiling, the stench of piss and other bodily fluids.

"Tell a billionaire that my brother is an addict and we're homeless? You would have thought I was after a handout."

"I could help."

"I don't need your pity."

"It's not pity, damn you, it's love."

The word has me gasping for air. My heart forgets to beat. I search his eyes to check if he's joking, playing a trick on the poor girl. But it's too dim in here to see.

"Let me love you, Chantelle. Let me take care of you."

The words are like a balm to my soul. To be taken care of. A memory flicks into my head of the warm shower, the mountain view and the man before me, laughing as I kick his ass at FIFA.

"But how can you love me? You're the Playboy of the Valley."

He runs a hand through his hair and lets out a long breath.

"That's a label some shitty journalist gave me. I'm not that guy anymore. I'm not sure I ever was that guy.

"I want more from life than celebrity status in trashy magazines. I thought hiding in the mountains was enough, but when I saw you, Chantelle, I knew you were mine. I just knew."

My heart's thundering in my ears. I don't see the playboy before me. I see the mountain rescuer, the kind man, the gentle man who healed me and looked after me and laughed with me. I see Alex.

"Why didn't you tell me who you were?"

"Because everyone who knows me from that past life wants a piece of me. For once, I met a woman who didn't know who I was, who I thought was into me for being me."

"I was. But our worlds are different, Alex. Look around you. I don't belong in your oversized mansion…cabin, whatever it is."

He catches my hand and pulls me toward him. "You belong with me, Chantelle."

Hope flutters in my stomach. I want to believe him, but that other life is just out of reach.

"I belong with Chris. He might be an addict. He might hurt me again, but he's the only family I have."

Alex frowns. "Was it him who hurt you on the trail?"

"Yes."

His eyes blaze. "When he sobers up, I'm going to kick his ass for that."

I shake my head and try to pull away. "You see, you don't understand. No matter what he does, I can't abandon him."

"And you don't understand." He jerks me towards him, his arm tight around my waist. "Your family is my family now, Chantelle. Your brother's a shit for doing that to you, and I'll kick his ass if he hurts you or anyone else again. But I have resources available to me. I'll get him the treatment he needs. I've already booked him into a private rehab center in the mountains. He'll have to do the hard work himself, but I'll help in the ways that I can."

I stare at him, unable to process it. "You'd do that for him?"

"He's your blood, Chantelle. I'll do it for you."

My eyes fill with tears. Chris will be getting out of here. That life I wanted; I can have it. Waking up next to a man I love, a roof over my head, food on the table, *safety.*

But something doesn't feel right.

"But…" I look around to the other poor souls, those less fortunate who don't have a rich benefactor.

Alex nods as if he can read my mind.

"I've established a trust to help tackle the drug epidemic in North Carolina. I'll need your help, if you want to do it with me, to figure out where the money is best spent."

I stare at him. "Are you offering me a job?"

"I'm offering you anything you want, Chantelle. A chance to help."

My mind races, already thinking of the possibilities. "There's a lack of funding for second tier rehab… then there's the mental health issues that are at the heart of addictive behavior…and trauma counselling for kids like Chris was…"

I spent many hours poring over library books, trying to get a better understanding of addiction and behavior. At one time I entertained a fantasy of going to college to be an adolescent psychologist to help people like Chris, whose addictive behaviors often start after a tragic event in childhood.

Alex pulls me to him. "Whatever you want, kitten."

I look into his kind eyes and realize that the only

thing I really want is to be with him. Because when I'm with him, everything else is possible.

Twelve months later…

Warm lips brush against the skin of my neck, making me shiver and drop my pencil.

"Hey."

I turn in my chair and swat at Alex playfully. "I'm trying to study."

He fixes me with a mischievous grin. "You're carrying around too much tension."

He pulls my chair away from the table and swivels it towards him, dropping to his knees in front of me. "I can't send you into an exam with all this tension."

His hands grip my thighs, sending an electric current through my body. I'm powerless to resist, and he's right. I'm tense.

I've got my first round of finals tomorrow and even though I've been studying every waking moment, I can't get rid of the anxiety that gnaws at me that it might not be enough.

"I suppose a quick break won't hurt."

He raises a bushy eyebrow at me. "Quick? Is that what you want, kitten?"

I bite my lower lip. My body's heating in all the places where our bodies are touching. Alex runs his fingers up my skirt and under my panties. I'm already slick for him, and he groans as he feels my need.

I'll take anything I can get from him, quick or slow.

"Stand up."

I do as I'm told, and Alex pulls my panties down and guides me over to the couch by the large window that looks out over the ravine and the valley beyond.

It's Miriam's day off, so when he bends me over the couch and flicks my skirt up, I comply without hesitation.

Alex sinks to his knees, and his lips trail up the back of my thighs. The heat of his mouth has me gripping the back of the couch. It's excruciatingly slow as his mouth travels upwards to my center of need.

I push my hips back as his mouth reaches my most sensitive parts.

He kisses around my pussy, licking me from slit to

slit, but keeping his touch away from the hard nub that quivers for a release.

I buck my hips backwards but he darts out of the way, making me mewl in frustration.

"What do you need, kitten?" he teases, as his thumb circles my slick folds.

I need him. I need release. I need something more than this exquisite torture.

"Please…"

I'm not above begging. Alex has all the power here, and all I can do is beg for what I need from him.

He chuckles, and his thumb presses on my puckered back entrance as his tongue finally strokes my clit.

I whimper against him as the pressure builds inside with every stroke.

His thumb pushes inside me while he licks me hard. And now I'm grinding into his face, mewling like a wild animal as he works me into a frenzy. Until the orgasm crashes over me, my body shuddering at the explosion of sensation.

I tremble on his hand, his tongue, his face, until Alex turns me around and kisses me hard, my pussy juices tangy on his tongue.

He pulls me around to the other side of the couch and lies me down on the plush rug. The stream burbles below us and the vast mountains watch silently as he mounts me, dragging my hips to him and thrusting inside. My legs wrap round his neck, and his thumb circles my clit.

We come together, with the mountains as our witness, in big shuddery orgasms.

My body flops on the rug afterwards, satisfied and spent. Alex was right. I needed to release the tension.

Afterwards, he makes me a hot chocolate and we sit curled up together, watching the sun turn orange over the valley.

After my exam tomorrow, we're going to visit Chris. He's been clean for six months and lives on the side of the mountain and works for the Best Life Foundation.

I never stop worrying about him, and his road to recovery isn't over yet. But he got the treatment he needed at the rehab center and counselling too, which he's still in. It takes a long time to unpack what he's been through, losing Mom and then the life of an addict.

He works at the organization distributing clothing and food and essentials to users. He's just started studying. He too wants to help, and we'll both be qualified counsellors in a few years' time.

"You two better get some sleep."

Alex rubs my belly and rests his hand on the firm skin there. The bump's not quite showing yet. We only found out a few weeks ago. I was worried about starting a family while I'm still studying, but Alex loves the idea. He can't wait to have children and swears he'll be the stay-at-home dad with the help of Miriam.

I lean back on him, my mountain rescuer, and warmth fills my heart. I never knew life could be like this for a girl like me. To be starting a family of my own, to be safe and belong.

Alex is my rock, my safe space, and I love him for that. I don't care who he was before. He'll always be my mountain rescuer.

GET YOUR BONUS SCENE

Want more Alex and Chantelle? Find out who's coming over for Sunday dinner in the bonus scene set ten years after their story finishes.

Sign up to the Sadie King mailing list and you'll get access to four free short romance ebooks plus all the bonus scenes.

You'll be the first to hear about new releases, exclusive offers, bonus content and all my news. You can even email me back. I love chatting with my readers!

To claim your free books visit:
authorsadieking.com/bonus-scenes

Already a subscriber? Check your last email for the link.

WHAT TO READ NEXT

MY MOUNTAIN MAN MILITARY HERO

Wild Heart Mountain is heating up when an ex-military hero meets his match with a young curvy volunteer firefighter.

Since being discharged from the military I've lost my purpose in life, until I find Erika…

She's feisty, curvy, and strong.

When we get stuck in a cabin together for the night, I'll show her that I might be a retired Special Forces captain, but I still know how to command…

My Mountain Man Military Hero is a forced proximity age gap instalove romance featuring an ex-military hero and an innocent curvy girl he claims as his own.

ABOUT THE AUTHOR

Sadie King is a USA Today Best Selling Author of contemporary romance novellas.

She lives in New Zealand with her ex-military husband and raucous young son.

When she's not writing she loves catching waves with her son, running along the beach, and drinking good wine with a book in hand.

Keep in touch when you sign up for her newsletter. You'll snag yourself a free short romance and access to all the bonus content!

authorsadieking.com/bonus-scenes

www.ingramcontent.com/pod-product-compliance
Lightning Source LLC
Chambersburg PA
CBHW021217130726
47988CB00002B/702